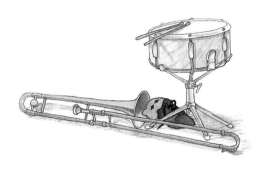

THIS WALKER BOOK BELONGS TO:

_____

_____

_____

First published 1989 by Walker Books Ltd
87 Vauxhall Walk, London SE11 5HJ

This edition published 2008

10 12 14 16 18 20 19 17 15 13 11

© 1989 Nick Butterworth

The right of Nick Butterworth to be identified as
author/illustrator of this work has been asserted by him in accordance
with the Copyright, Designs and Patents Act 1988

This book has been typeset in New Century School Book

Printed in China

British Library Cataloguing in Publication Data:
a catalogue record for this book is available from the British Library

ISBN 978-1-4063-1330-7

www.walker.co.uk

My Dad is
BRILLIANT

Nick Butterworth

WALKER BOOKS
AND SUBSIDIARIES
LONDON • BOSTON • SYDNEY • AUCKLAND

My dad is
brilliant.

He's as
strong as a
gorilla …

and he can
run like a
cheetah ...

and he can
play any
instrument ...

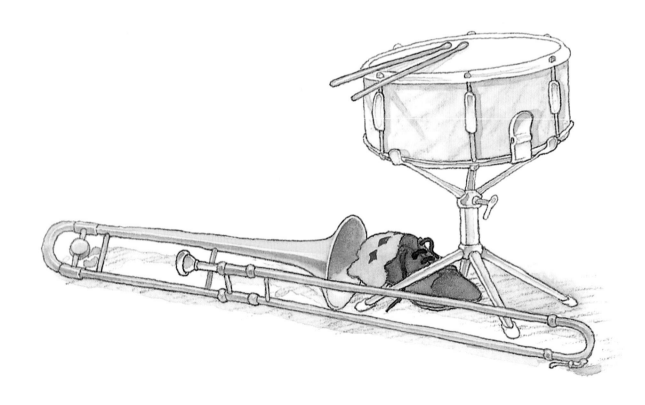

and he's
a marvellous
cook ...

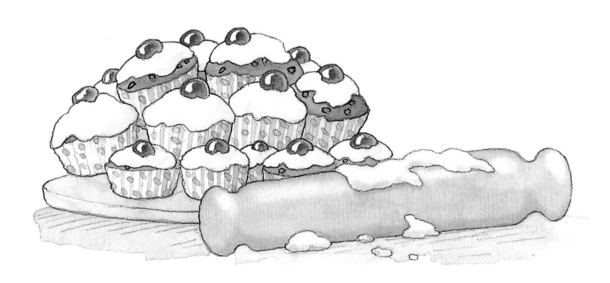

and he's
fantastic on
roller skates…

and he's
brilliant at making
things …

and he can
sing like a
pop star …

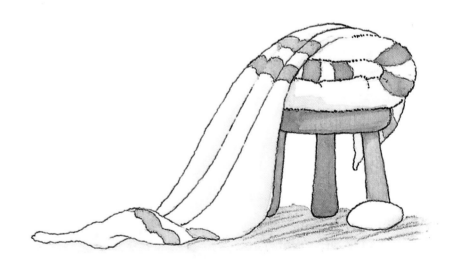

and he can
juggle with
anything ...

and he's not
a bit frightened
of the dark …

and he tells the
funniest jokes
in the world.

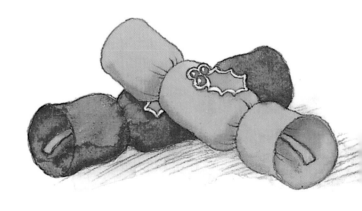

It's great to
have a dad
like mine.

It's brilliant!

Other titles by Nick Butterworth

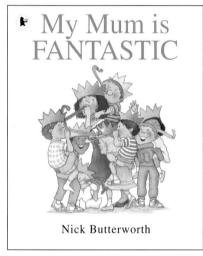

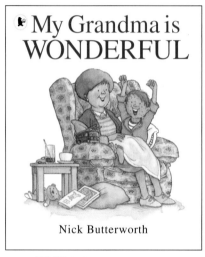

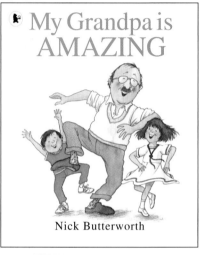

ISBN 978-1-4063-1242-3 ISBN 978-1-4063-1243-0 ISBN 978-1-4063-1331-4

"I wonder how much time I spent as a boy singing the praises of my family.
My grandpa could make *anything* out of *anything*. My grandma was the
best friend anyone could ever wish for. My dad was little short of Superman
and my mum ... well, perhaps she actually *was* Wonderwoman!
It's heartening to know that children feel the same today
as I did then. Especially my own two!"

NICK BUTTERWORTH

Available from all good bookstores

www.walkerbooks.co.uk